I0648775

Unitarian Congregational Society

Samuel Joseph May

Born in Boston, Massachusetts 1797

Unitarian Congregational Society

Samuel Joseph May
Born in Boston, Massachusetts 1797

ISBN/EAN: 9783337283063

Printed in Europe, USA, Canada, Australia, Japan

Cover: Foto ©Raphael Reischuk / pixelio.de

More available books at **www.hansebooks.com**

SAMUEL JOSEPH MAY.

BORN IN BOSTON, MASSACHUSETTS,

September 12th, 1797.

DIED IN SYRACUSE, NEW YORK,

July 1st, 1871.

—

SYRACUSE:
PRINTED AT THE JOURNAL OFFICE,
1871.

" *And I heard a voice from Heaven, saying unto me, Write, Blessed are the dead which die in the Lord from henceforth: yea saith the Spirit, that they may rest from their labors ; and their works do follow them.*"

Another hand is beckoning us,
    Another call is given,
And glows once more with angel steps
    The path which reaches Heaven.

* * * *

Sweet promptings unto kindest deeds
    Were in his very look ;
We read his face, as one who reads
    A true and holy book ;

The measure of a blessed hymn
    To which our hearts could move ;
The breathing of an inward psalm,
    A canticle of love.

* * * *

Fold him, O Father, in Thine arms,
    And let him henceforth be
A messenger of love, between
    Our human hearts and Thee.

Still let his mild rebuking stand
    Between us and the wrong,
And his dear memory serve to make
    Our faith in goodness strong.

INTRODUCTORY.

At a meeting of the members of the Unitarian Congregational Society of Syracuse, held after morning service in the Church of the Messiah, on Sunday, July 9th, 1871, a committee, consisting of Rev. S. R. Calthrop, Mr. C. D. B. Mills, Mr. D. P. Phelps, Mr. H. N. White, Mrs. Mary E. Bagg, and Mrs. Rebecca J. Burt, was appointed to prepare and publish a memorial pamphlet embracing the funeral obsequies of the former pastor of the Society,—Rev. Samuel J. May.

In the performance of that duty, the committee have not thought it advisable to use more of the very abundant matter in their hands, than is included in the following pages. They were inclined at first, to add some of the very many appreciative and glowing tributes to Mr. May's life and character which his death spontaneously called out, from both the religious and secular press.

The occasion seemed also to invite a somewhat detailed account of his pastorate in Syracuse, so faithfully filled on the one hand and so lovingly received on the other—extending from 1845 to 1868—through twenty-three of the best years of his active, beautiful and saintly life, and which was officially ended, only to be merged in new relations with his people, if possible stronger and more tender than before.

But upon reflection it was felt, that a rounded Christian life like Mr. May's—so beautiful and complete in all its full proportions, called at once for a faithful and loving biographer, and that any attempt on the part of the committee to anticipate in this memorial of his death and burial, any material part of that biographer's proper work, would be inappropriate. By whomsoever the story of his life shall be told, we may rest assured that his pastorate in Syracuse, and the noble work which he here did for his parish, for the community about him, and for the world at large, will receive the attention which it deserves.

And yet the committee have deemed it very proper to go so far beyond the limitation thus marked out for themselves, as to incorporate in this memorial, the very full obituary notice of Mr. May which appeared in the *Syracuse Daily Standard*, on the Monday morning after his death ; a notice which for its brief comprehensiveness, its thorough appreciation of the work he had done and of his exalted christian character, and for its loving tenderness of spirit and expression, seemed to make it the fitting article for the place we give it.

The committee have also to express their obligations to the several daily papers of the city, and to the *Christian Register* of Boston, for their very full reports of the services at the Church and at Oakwood, on the occasion of the funeral, of which they have very freely availed themselves.

The death of Mr. May was quite sudden. Although he had been ill for several weeks, he felt much better again, and spoke hopefully of dismissing his nurse, and of visiting New England. He saw several friends on Saturday, including President White, of Cornell University, who informed him of an offer received by his University of a very liberal gift, upon the condition that young women should have the same advantages as young men in that institution. Mr. May promised to give the college his portrait of Prudence Crandall, if this should be consummated, and he parted with Mr. White in the most cheerful and affectionate manner. About ten o'clock in the evening he became very ill. As his strength ebbed away, he manifested a desire that his daughter should kiss him, and then, with a farewell smile his spirit took its upward flight.

His death occurred at so late an hour on Saturday evening, that but few persons knew of it until announced, as it was, in several of the churches after morning service next day.

These announcements were generally accompanied by spontaneous, heartfelt tributes to his exalted character and pure, noble life.

The whole community were deeply impressed ; and as soon as it became generally known, large numbers of persons—people of all conditions in life—called at the house of his son-in-law, Mr. Alfred Wilkinson, with whom he had lived, not only to express their respect and sorrow, but that they might once more look upon that face, which in death retained the same beautiful expression of love for all his kind, which made it everywhere and always in life, a welcome presence, shedding heavenly benedictions upon all around him. And so, to the day of his funeral, friends from far and near, those who knew him well and those who only knew of him, came there, impelled by a common sorrow, which had cast its dark shadow over all their homes, and made deep wounds in all their hearts.

Gerrit Smith came from Peterboro, notwithstanding his own illness, and also wrote: "Mr. May was the most Christ-like man that I ever knew. He made Christ his pattern, and how successfully, was proved by his never-failing gentleness, meekness and sweetness. Heaven is more desirable to me now that my dear May is there."

The city papers of Monday morning, contained long and glowing tributes to his worth, one of which, from the *Daily Standard*, we reproduce.

SAMUEL JOSEPH MAY.

Not in this community alone, where the kindly face of our departed friend and teacher was so familiarly known, and his reputation so tenderly cherished, but also in many different sections of the land, where he had worked in holy enterprises, and attached to himself zealous circles of friends, will the announcement of the death of Samuel J. May be received with profoundest sorrow. In common with a host of loving ones, impressed with the sublimity of the character we would depict, and the worthlessness of words in its serene presence, we would offer our tribute of respect to the memory of him who, through goodness, rose to greatness, uniting the courage of a Knox and the ardor of a Howard with the dear simplicity of the Vicar of Wakefield. The life we would sketch was unusually prolonged and essentially earnest, crowded with activities and crowned with blessings; and it is, therefore, difficult, in a limited space, to compass a comprehensive survey of its usefulness, or even to detail many of the facts which gave it significance; nor does this, indeed, seem necessary in a region which sensitively vibrated to its touch, and is imbued with regard for its efficacy and reverence for its spirit. We trust, however, that we may be enabled, while outlining its course, to emphasize a portion of its virtues and to extract therefrom something of the secret of its power.

Samuel Joseph May was born in Boston on the 12th day of September, 1797. He was the tenth of twelve children of Joseph and Dorothy Sewall May, all of whom attained mature years, and but one of whom, the wife of the thinker Alcott, and the mother of the author of " Little Women," survives. He was of Puritan stock, as moulded by the hardy influences of early colonial times and as modified by the searching theological reformation which swept over Massachusetts towards the close of the last century. He was descended, in the fourth generation, from John May, who, born in England in 1628, came to New England while quite a lad, settled in Roxbury, near Jamaica Pond, and acquired an estate which remained in the family so late as 1810. No circumstances could be more conducive to a true mental and moral development, and no happier ties of kindred could exist than those which waited on the opening years of Samuel J. May. He was allied to the best blood of his native state—historic in the grand old Commonwealth. His mother was the daughter of Samuel Sewall, of Boston, by his wife, Elizabeth Quincy, niece of Josiah Quincy, Jr., of glorious memory, and sister of the wife of John Hancock. She was the lineal descendant of Chief Justice Sewall, of Salem, one of the first to suspect, and finally to expose the Witchcraft delusion. She was also the sister of a later Chief Justice, and the grand-daughter of the Rev. Joseph Sewall, pastor for many years of the Old South Church, a Calvinist divine of justly extended reputation.

Joseph May, the father, designed to study for the ministry, but was prevented from so doing by the breaking out of the Revolutionary war. He engaged in business pursuits, was Colonel of Militia in the famous "Boston Cadets," and Secretary, for forty years, of one of the earliest organized Marine Insurance Companies in the country, and was highly esteemed for his integrity, exactness and charitable energies. He lived until 1841, dying at the age of eighty-one. As related to the religious bias and labors of his son, the most interesting feature of his career was his connection, for nearly half a century, with King's Chapel, as one of its Wardens and most tenacious supporters. King's Chapel, left without a priest, by the flight of its tory incumbent, invited the Rev. James Freeman to conduct, as a Reader, its services. At the close of the Revolution, he was solicited to become its Rector, but upon applying to the Bishop for ordination, was unable to subscribe to the Thirty-Nine articles, as well as to certain observances of the Episcopal establishment, and being tinctured with the reputed heresies of Priestley, was denied the sacred rite. His congregation, nevertheless, endorsed his views, and themselves installed him. Thus was instituted the first Unitarian Church in America, to which Dr. Freeman ministered until his death in 1835, and Col. May gave his consistent aid, and from which Samuel J. received inspiration and instruction. Of the value of his early religious education Mr. May had the liveliest appreciation. He held it as one of the chief blessings of his life that he was not devoted to the tenets of a stern creed and the terrible imaginings it imposes. He was a Liberal Christian, almost by intuition ; and hence experienced none of the pangs with which the conflict between the dogma of vengeance and the gospel of love tortures so many souls.

Mr. May received his education, preliminary to entering college, at the Chauncy Hall School, famous for many years in Boston, and still flourishing. He entered Harvard College in the fall of 1813, and graduated in 1817, with high rank in a class which has since, in many of its members, proved itself illustrious. Among its notable names are those of George Bancroft, Caleb Cushing, Samuel A. Eliot, member of Congress from Massachusetts, and the father of President Eliot, George B. Emerson, a leading teacher and student of natural and social science, Samuel E. Sewall, a distinguished lawyer of Boston and cousin and chum of Mr May, the Rev. Dr. Stephen H. Tyng, and the Rev. Dr. Alvah Woods. The late Dr. Holyoke, of this city, was also a class-mate; and in this connection we should not omit to mention one who achieved an ignoble fame— Robert Schuyler, the great defaulter. It is noteworthy that in 1869, fifty two years after graduation, nearly one-half of this class of sixty-seven members was alive—a convincing proof of its average moral worth. At the termination of his academic course, and indeed before, Mr. May engaged in teaching at Hingham, Concord, Beverly and Nahant, pursuing meantime his classical and theological studies, and becoming aroused to that deep interest in the cause of popular education which he ever maintained. Among his pupils at Nahant was the historian Motley, whom he instructed in the English language. if not in that of " the Dutch Republic." In the spring of 1818, he entered the Divinity School at Cambridge, graduating in 1820, and he was approbated to preach in December of that year. The School was then under charge of Dr. Henry Ware, Sen., who was assisted by Professors Norton, Frisbie and Willard, all clear-headed, keen-sighted and conscientious instructors. Of the manner of their teaching Mr. May gives the following exposition : " These gentlemen marked out for us a sufficiently extended theological, as well as ethical and devotional course of reading; but they peremptorily *dictated* nothing except personal purity and righteousness, the diligent improvement of our advantages, and fidelity to our highest sense of the true and the right. They enjoined it upon us to examine every subject brought to our consideration thoroughly and as impartially as we were able in the various lights thrown upon it by the religious and theological writers of opposite sects, and to accept such conclusions as should, after such an examination, seem to our minds correct—remembering our responsibility to God alone, for the use we made of our opportunities to learn, and of the powers He had given us to judge of the true and the right."

As indicative of the effect of such counsels upon himself we continue our quotation from the discourse delivered in the Church of the Messiah, in 1867, upon the occasion of his reaching his seventieth birthday: "Thus encouraged I entered upon the inquiry after *true religion*, fully persuaded that it was the 'one thing needful' for all men; and longing to be a minister of it to my fellow beings, so many of whom seemed to me to be 'living without God in the world.' I was soon more than ever convinced that Christianity was the true religion; but that a strange theology had been foisted into its place in Christendom; substituted for it in most of the churches. It seemed to me self-evident, that Christianity was to be learnt from Jesus Christ; that he must be the best teacher of his own religion; that, if he be, as most Christians profess to regard him, 'the author and *finisher* of our faith,' nothing should be *appended* to the Gospel as he left it; not even on the authority of Paul, Appollos, or Cephas; certainly not on the authority of St. Augustine, John Calvin, or the Pope, should anything be prescribed as essential, which is not perfectly consistent with the teaching of the Master. It seemed to me then, as it seems to me now, the highest impertinence, and most egregious presumption, in any Doctor of Divinity, Assembly of Divines (especially those who believe that Jesus was a superhuman being, aye, the very God), to prescribe a Creed, as comprising the essential faith, which is nowhere to be found in the words of the Master."

Thus holding to personal purity of life, and placing himself in the attitude of a seeker after truth, under the All-Father, he commenced the work of the ministry, serving as supply at Springfield, Mass., Brooklyn, Connecticut, and New York City, during the succeeding year. In 1821, he made a journey to Richmond, Va., preaching on his way at Baltimore, Washington, and other cities. In Washington, that abhorrence of "the peculiar institution," which soon became one of the strongest impulses of his life, as displayed in acts of daring and devotion, was aroused by seeing a coffle of slaves in the street. Returning to Boston, he became the temporary colleague of Dr. Channing, in the Federal street pulpit, and in this connection continued several months. The intercourse with this gifted and fervent apostle of Liberal Christianity had a most energizing and sanctifying influence upon the ministrations of Mr. May, and he was accustomed to refer to it as of eminent benefit to him in many respects. Upon his part, Dr. Channing conceived a warm friendship for his youthful assistant, and maintained it until his death, delighting always to welcome and to counsel with him, even at times when their views upon public questions were somewhat divergent. While he was in Boston, he was invited to gather a church at Richmond, Virginia, and was strongly tempted to an enterprise which seemed to have many encouraging prospects; but receiving a simultaneous call to Brooklyn, Conn., where was located the only Unitarian Church in that state, he deemed it his duty to accept the latter invitation. He had previously been ordained to the ministry by the Association of Boston churches, the ceremony being notable from the high standing of the clergymen who officiated in it. It took place in Chauncy Place Church, March 13th, 1822, the Rev. Dr. Freeman preaching the sermon, the Rev. Dr. Channing giving the charge, the Rev. Dr. Greenwood extending the right hand of Fellowship, and the Rev. Henry Ware, Jr., making the prayer of Ordination. On the succeeding Sabbath he took charge of the church at Brooklyn; from which time his settled labors in the ministry may be said to date.

He lived in Brooklyn fourteen years, bringing a feeble church into a state of efficiency, impressing his personality upon his neighbors, and being prominently identified with every good work to which he could put his hand. Besides fulfilling the ordinary duties of his parish, he edited a paper called *The Liberal Christian*, was a member of the School Committee of the town, and did much to raise the standard of education in the state, giving lectures on the subject, and calling the first convention ever held to consider the question of popular education. He early took ground in favor of a less austere and more rational use of Sunday, against exclusiveness in the administration of the Lord's Supper, and against ritualistic methods in the church, discarding in a short time after his ordination the gown and bands then universally worn; but an aged man having scruples about baptism, and believing on Scripture grounds that immersion was necessary to the validity of the rite, he consented to gratify his desire by entering a river with him, but addressed the meeting on coming out to the effect that a drop of water was sufficient to baptize a man whose heart was really consecrated, an ocean otherwise having no potency. At this time, as always, his characteristic doctrine was that no form, or service, or profession, makes a man acceptable to God, but only the denying of all ungodliness and living soberly, righteously and piously in all the relations of life—in an adherence, so far as possible, to the precept of the Golden Rule.

At Brooklyn Mr. May became actively interested also in the various reforms to which he afterwards gave so much of his thought and strength, and to which we shall hereafter allude, as a biography of him without including something of them would be singularly incomplete. On the first of June, 1825, he married Lucretia Flagge Coffin, daughter of Peter Coffin, a merchant of Boston, and had issue by her as follows:—Joseph, died in infancy; John Edward, now in business in Boston; Charlotte Coffin, wife of Alfred Wilkinson, of this city; Joseph, minister of the Unitarian Church in Newburyport, Mass.; and George Emerson, engaged in mercantile pursuits. The wedded life of Mr. May, was, we need not say, beautiful in the blended being of kindred souls—redolent with the perfume of affection, and blossoming in the sweetest charities. Mrs. May, known, honored, and loved in this community, has but recently passed away. Gentle in disposition, retiring in manners, yet highly cultured, firm in purpose, and thoroughly sympathizing with the aims of her husband, her kindly influence was felt in every circle in which she moved, and her supreme confidence in the righteousness of his labors sensibly nerved him to persevere in their behalf.

He resigned from Brooklyn in 1835 to accept the position

of general agent of the Massachusetts Anti Slavery Society, in which he continued eighteen months, lecturing, writing and arranging conventions. Late in 1836, he was installed over the church at South Scituate, Plymouth county, Mass., remaining there for six years. He at once took up his work in the same active and practical spirit which had before marked it. Under his administration the prosperity of the church was greatly enhanced, spiritually and temporally. Already recognized as a reformer, he continued his labors for Anti-Slavery, Peace, Temperance, Education and other worthy objects of his zeal. His house was the rendezvous for reformers of all kinds. Garrison, Phillips, Foster, Pillsbury, Abby Kelly, Lucretia Mott, Douglass, Remond were all at home in the Scituate parsonage. He was the intimate friend and adviser of Horace Mann; he organized societies for reform purposes, held anti-slavery conventions and temperance meetings, and lectured all through the eastern part of Massachusetts. Plymouth county he regarded as his parish, and was personally known and esteemed in all parts of it. At the same time, he was indefatigable in his ministerial work, an affectionate and devoted pastor; his memory is still green and fresh in the little town; and his visits to it, which have been frequent of late, have always been in the nature of ovations.

In 1842, the position of principal of the Normal School for female teachers at Lexington having became vacant through the illness of the incumbent, Hon. Horace Mann, then Secretary of the State Board of Education, urged the place upon Mr. May, and he accepted it, removing immediately to Lexington and assuming control of the school; but, within two years, the former principal recovering his health, Mr. May, though honored and useful in, and attached to the position, resigned in his favor, feeling it to be the right

of his predecessor to be reinstated. He was then invited
to the charge of the Lexington parish and accepted the
same temporarily. The church stood on sacred ground,
within the region where the first fighting of the Revolution
occurred, on the common where the villagers mustered to
meet the red-coats and where the first volley of battle was
fired. The spirit of conflict was not yet dead within the
town. Theological differences raged within it, and Mr.
May was called to a duty he often had to perform—the
duty of peace-maker. A feud had completely alienated the
sympathies of the two parishes into which the town was di-
vided, growing out of a dispute concerning the proper distribution of a church fund. Mr. May's was the old parish
and (as is usual in the old towns of New England) had become Unitarian, the adherents to the evangelical creed
having seceded to form a new church. So bitter was the
hostility of the two organizations that social amenities
were almost disregarded among them. Mr. May, with that
desire for peace which was one of his most prominent characteristics, at once applied himself to the settlement of this
quarrel, and labored so successfully as to procure an equi-
table adjustment of the matters in difference and a reconc lia-
tion of the people. " Blessed are the peace-makers, for they
shall be called the children of God."

While Mr. May lived in Lexington there arose, in Boston,
the famous Theodore Parker, then the leading thinker of
the now so-called Radical theologians. Parker was, as is
well known, though the minister of a Unitarian parish,
completely ostracised by the clergy of Boston and treated
by them in a manner particularly inconsistent with their
peculiar gospel of personal mental freedom. Their conduct
roused the indignation of Mr. May, who, at that time, coinci-
ded in the theological views of Mr. Parker less clearly than
at a later period ; but he was sincere in his profession of be-

lief that every man must be fully persuaded in his own mind and had a right to speak his thought. He wrote to Mr. Parker, expressing his sympathy with him and proposing an exchange of pulpits. Herein the broadness of that charity, which was the crowning grace of our friend's character, thus early declared itself. Only two other Unitarian clergymen were as true to the principle of free thought as this. The result of Mr. May's proffer was a friendship close, affectionate and firm, which endured so long as Mr. Parker lived.

At the conclusion of his temporary engagement with the church of Lexington, Mr. May received an invitation from the school committee of Boston to become head master of one of its public schools. This offered him a favorable opportunity to embrace a profession congenial to his taste and in which he had already distinguished himself. He strongly desired so to do, but was willing to consent only on the condition that his school should be excepted from the operation of the "Franklin Medal" system, receiving, in lieu of the medals awarded for distribution in each school, an equivalent in money to be used in a way he should deem less objectionable. The committee replied, expressing their sympathy in his objections to this method of stimulation, but stating that the laws left them no discretion as to the Franklin Fund. He therefore declined the offer.

In 1843, Mr. May made a journey to Niagara, accompanied by his wife, and was invited by the Rev. Mr. Storer, first pastor of the Unitarian Church in Syracuse, to occupy his pulpit for several Sundays. He thus became known to the members of this congregation, and, upon Mr. Storer's death, which sudden circumstance is vividly remembered by many of our citizens, was invited first to preach as a candidate and then to become its pastor—with what unanimity the following letter attests :—

This call Mr. May accepted and preached for the first time as pastor of the church sometime in the April succeeding. The church, to which he was thus called, was as yet in its infancy, although its membership embraced some of the strongest men of the village. It was organized in 1837, embracing among its founders such names as E. F. Wallace, John Wilkinson, Hiram Putnam, John Newell, Parley Bassett, Aaron Burt, Joseph Savage, J. L. Bagg, D. P. Phelps, D. J. Morris, B. F. Colvin, C. F. Williston, James G. Tracy, M. M. White, E. J. Foster, Coddington B. Williams, Stephen Smith, Jared H. Parker and H. N. White. The Rev. J. P. B. Storer, a highly intellectual and much loved clergyman, had been its pastor from 1839 until his death, of heart disease, in the summer of 1844. Originally worshipping in a little wooden chapel on East Genesee street, on or near the site of the present Seymour Block, it had, in 1843, removed to a new and pleasant edifice on its present lot which, with additions and enlargements, lasted until it was destroyed by the falling of the spire in 1852, the present church being completed in 1853.

It was not to be expected that a new-coming Unitarian minister would receive a cordial welcome from the clergymen whose opposition had much tried the less resolute heart of his predecessor. Nor did he ; but to such opposition he was already accustomed, and for it was fully prepared. He took up his ministerial work with good heart, and met the sermons occasionally preached in denunciation of his theological position with pretty constant expositions of what he found objectionable and abhorrent in the popular creeds ; and it was not long before his utter geniality conquered the hearts. if it did not change the convictions, of his Orthodox brethren. With the late Dr. Adams, who had strongly denounced him, he, at last, contracted a friendship, sincere if not very demonstrative, and the good Doctor, upon his death-bed, sent for him and they had a long conference, a fact to which Mr. May was accustomed to refer with truly Christian pride.

Of his pastoral labors we need not speak at length. In the hearts of his hearers they are forever enshrined. Under his watchful care, the church has steadily and gradually grown into a power in our midst. He has gone out and in among its members for twenty-six years, blessing their children, marrying their young men and maidens, committing their dust to solemn sepulture—by all of them respected, loved, venerated as it has been the fortune of few pastors. in this age of the decadence of respect for the ministerial office, to be honored. Not a great pulpit orator, he was yet a singularly clear writer, with terse and vigorous sentences often infused into the plainness of a narrative style. He rose ever to the eloquence of earnestness, and none might doubt the sincerity of the thought which guided his pen. In every house of his parish he was a welcome guest ; received rather with the warmth of regard which marks the affinity of blood. Thus strong in the pulpit and loved on the hearth stone, he filled the years of his usefulness in the ministry until the lengthening shadows of his life compelled him to decline its further responsibilities. On the 15th of September, 1867, he tendered to the church his resignation,—which was accepted on the 7th of October, with resolutions of the deepest respect and affection, a liberal annuity being voted him to take effect when his successor should be installed.   This was accomplished on the 29th of April, 1868, when the Rev. Mr. Calthrop was received as pastor.   On the 15th of September, 1867, upon the completion of his seventieth year, he preached "A Brief Account of his Ministry," to which we are indebted for many of the facts and suggestions of this biography, and from which we may be permitted to make a further quotation, as illustrating, in a small compass, the character of his ministry.

"Thus it was, dear friends, that an acquaintance commenced twenty-four years ago last month, which led to my settlement with you in April, 1845, as your minister.   What sort of a minister I should probably be, you were fairly warned, for during my visits, in 1843, and again during the four weeks that I preached to you as a candidate, in November and December, 1844, I lectured in the city twice on the immediate abolition of slavery ; once, on the paramount importance of an improved system of popular education ; and once, if I remember correctly, on the great expediency, if not duty, of total abstinence from the use of any intoxicating drinks.   Therefore, if you have been much disappointed in the character of my ministry here, you must blame your own want of discernment and not any concealment on my part." It may well be added that while it was a bold undertaking for a minister in this State, a quarter of a century ago, thus unreservedly to identify himself with these obnoxious reforms, in this church no root of bitterness was planted by the efforts of its pastor; on the contrary he nurtured and tended the seed of his own sowing within it, and from a fruitful soil it sprang up and bore abundant fruit. No church can claim greater credit for efficient humanitarian labors than the Unitarian Society of Syracuse. He educated it up to his own standards.

We have said that any sketch of Mr. May's life would be singularly incomplete without an allusion to his connection with the great reforms of the day. Herein he was a pioneer and acquired a national reputation; his philanthropy was of the purest and most enlarged type; but we may do little more than allude to it; for, even if our space did not forbid a larger reference, we know that there are many intimately associated with him in various progressive movements who will do him fuller justice than we may hope to do, and who will be swift to bear their testimony to the worth of his counsels and the completeness of his consecration. He was among the apostles of the gospel of anti-slavery. His disgust at the abuses of slavery, incited by personal observation of its enormities, developed, under the inspiration of William Lloyd Garrison, into an undying hostility towards the institution of barbarism. So early as 1830 he preached anti-slavery sermons, to the annoyance of his good friends, Dr. Channing and the Rev. Henry Ware, Jr., and to the alarm of his father. He defended Prudence Crandall against an indictment, under a modern Connecticut "blue law," for teaching a school to which colored children were admitted. He was the agent, as we have shown, for nearly two years of the Massachusetts anti-slavery society, during which connection he was grievously persecuted for opinion's sake, being on several occasions mobbed—notably at Newburyport and Haverhill—and to our disgrace, be it said, burned in effigy in this city so late as 1861. He was a prominent member—and very proud was he of that membership—of the Convention at Philadelphia which instituted the American Anti-Slavery Society, to whose constitution, on the 6th of December, 1833, sixty-one devoted men signed their names. He was one of the sub-committee which drafted the famous declaration of anti-slavery purpose, William Lloyd Garrison and John G. Whittier being the other members, the principal labor of composition being confided to Mr. Garrison. Thenceforth, Mr. May was one of the most earnest anti-slavery advocates in the land, speaking from pulpit and from rostrum upon every occasion when God gave him grace and man gave him an opportunity. No convention was complete without his presence, and no council chamber of the fiery-hearted leaders but relied upon his wisdom. His house was a principal depot of the underground railroad, and to his protection many hundreds of panting fugitives were consigned, whom he guided safely to a haven of rest and freedom, often after ministering to their pecuniary necessities from his slender purse. Man of peace though he was, he became implicated in the rescue of the slave "Jerry," and, despising the law under which the iniquity of rendition was possible, would willingly have suffered stripes and imprisonment for the release of even the humblest bondmen. In 1869, he published a volume entitled, "Some Recollections of the Anti-Slavery Conflict," which has had an extensive circulation, and is full of information concerning the trials of those earnest men to whom, under God, the nation is indebted for its deliverance from the burden of its sin.

Mr. May had become interested in the question of peace while at College, by listening to addresses from Dr. Noah Worcester, and steadily bore his testimony against the necessity of war according to the convictions he then acquired. In 1826 he formed an Auxiliary Peace Society in Brooklyn, to co-operate with that of Dr. Worcester; and being elected chaplain of a Connecticut regiment, he declined the honor, telling the Colonel " he could not pray that they might do the very thing they would be mustered to do—but only that they might beat their swords into plow-shares and learn war no more." The first pamphlet he ever published was an " Exposition of the Sentiments and Purposes of the Windham County Peace Society," in 1826. It is believed, however, that his sentiments upon this subject became somewhat modified when secession culminated in treason and the nation rose to its feet to confront the foe in its own household.

At an early day, also, he become opposed to capital punishment. Being waited on by a sheriff to be present at the execution of an atrocious murderer, he enquired if the condemned desired him to attend, and upon being told that he was invited on behalf of the State, he answered that he would not attend ; he would go if the criminal requested it, as the sympathizing friend of a very wicked brother, but would in no way seem to countenance the State in doing what he thought the State had no right to do. The conversation which followed so impressed the Sheriff that he declined to act as the executioner. Against judicial murder Mr. May remained constantly opposed during the rest of his life, preaching and writing against its enormity.

In May, 1826, he attended the Boston Anniversaries and was present at a meeting of the Massachusetts Temperance Society, as also at a meeting of Unitarian ministers called to consider the subject of temperance. He had not previously regarded it as wrong to drink wine in moderation, but was so much influenced by these discussions that he determined to discountenance the use of all intoxicants,— "lest he should cause his brother to offend." Returning home he received the hearty sympathy of his wife, and soon called public attention to the subject. He personally visited every retailer of liquors in the town, to ascertain the amounts of liquor sold, and from the overseers of the poor, physicians and others, learned something of the disastrous effects of the traffic. The result was the adoption, under his leadership, by many individuals, of the rule of Total Abstinence and the formation of a society having its principles in view. Of his labors in this city in this direction we all know personally. He was one of the staunchest friends of this reform, joining a number of organizations pledged to its support, and one of his last public addresses was in its advocacy, before the Syracuse Christian Union, the address being published by its request in this journal.

Latterly he had become much interested in the demand of Woman for Suffrage and interested himself in its enforcement with all the fire of his youth. Of the immense labor all these reforms necessitated, of the travels, the correspondence, both foreign and domestic, of the numbers of speeches delivered, we have no reliable data. We know, however, that his activities were severely taxed to the very end, and that he had laid out an amount of work, literary and otherwise, which would have appalled an ordinary man of half his years. It is certainly to be regretted that an autobiography, which he had in contemplation, remains in an unfinished state. Mr. May had published much of a secular and religious cast; but little of it, however, in permanent form. His last publication was a pamphlet entitled "A Complaint against the Presbyterians and their Confession of Faith," which is very perspicuously written and is valuable as giving evidence of the maintenance of his life-long views of the goodness of God.

To write of Mr. May as a citizen is a grateful task. He was a minister who came out of his pulpit to mingle with his fellow men, bringing the meditations of the closet and the soul of good-will to bear upon the social problems which beset us all. He came to us when we were a village; he lived among us to see our population quintupled—a fair and prosperous city. He was as public-spirited as philanthropic. No improvement but had his sanction, no charity but had his encouragement. The Franklin Institute, the Historical Association, the Orphan Asylum, the Home, the Hospital, all called him their friend. No differing creed could deter him from giving his aid to a noble enterprise. At our public meetings he was often present, whatever their object—provided only it was commendable. His charities flowed in all directions—towards the Indians of our Reservation, the homeless boys who wander along our great artery of inland navigation, the victims of self-imposed or heaven-sent wretchedness at our doors.

We have spoken of Mr. May's interest in the cause of popular education, elsewhere; it was here signally exhibited and, we believe, fully appreciated. Those of us, who were at school twenty years ago, remember how often his genial face beamed in upon our studies, and his words of advice encouraged us in our pursuits. Many of us then learned to love him—a love which has not been diminished by constant acts of kindness and of countenance since received. In 1864 he was elected, from the fourth ward, member of the Board of Education and by successive and unanimous re-elections continued therein for the ensuing six years. During the last five years of his service he was President of the Board. He was faithful in attendance at its meetings and judicious in his selection of its committees. He was thoroughly acquainted with the discipline and the studies of the schools, and with the character and qualifications of their teachers. He gave much of his time to a personal inspection of the schools, not only of his own ward, but also of the whole city, and his was ever a welcome presence in the school room. He was greatly interested in the High School, and to him is largely due the erection of its present magnificent building, and the comprehensive range of studies there pursued. He strenuously opposed corporal punishment, here as everywhere, and to no man in the country may greater credit be awarded for the gentler modes of correction which have nearly banished the fools cap and the birch from systems of education. As a memorial of his labors the " May School " was named in his honor by his associates—and, we believe, he would ask for no more suitable monument. Nor should we forget the interest he manifested in the education of the very littil ones, the " Kindergarten " system particularly commending itself to his judgment, as a promising advance upon the arbitrary methods yet in vogue.

And now, as we write our last words, we would if possible have our pen touched, as by an angel, to fitly note the gracious character itself of which the record we have sketched is but the outward expression ; but words are cold and speech is lifeless here. There was no man of truer convictions, of more generous impulses, of a nobler self-abandonment than he. His charities were as countless as the dewdrops glistening on the meadows of morning ; his sympathies as pervasive as the objects towards which they could be directed. A zealot, he had none of the zealot's bitterness ; a reformer, he had not the reformer's caustic tongue ; a theologian of pronounced views, he had none of the theologian's regard for sect. True to his own flesh and blood, he was yet everybody's friend. Simple in his habits, confiding in his nature, sometimes imposed upon through the very excess of his philanthropy, no man but respected him for the possession of the most sterling qualities of head as well as of heart. Now that the asperities of the conflicts in which he was engaged are hushed in the triumph of nearly all the principles for which he contended, we believe there is no man living who will cherish an envious or a hostile feeling over this new-made grave. Utterly free from envy himself, he paid most generous tribute to the talents and the good works of his fellows. In the fullness of years, with intellect unimpaired, with affections undiminished, with a record lustrous for its accomplishment and beautiful in its spirit, with the regard of all who had heard of him, and the veneration of all who knew him, he has been gathered to the fathers, and taken his place among that goodly company who " by pureness, by knowledge, by long suffering, by kindness, by the Holy Ghost, by love unfeigned, by the word of truth, by the power of God, by the armor of righteousness on the right hand and on the left, by honor and dishonor, by evil report and good report," have entered into the rest of the faithful. To use his own words, he had learned life's lesson, and had gladly turned the page to see what there is on the other side. Upon us his life falls like a benediction, gracious and gentle, from the hands of the Father Supreme. May it be given us to live as in its presence, and to assimilate in our characters something of its essence !

SOCIETY TESTIMONIALS.

MEETING OF THE MEMBERS OF THE CHURCH OF THE MESSIAH.

A very largely attended meeting of the members of the Church of the Messiah and of that Society, was held Monday evening July 3d, to take action in regard to the death of the late Rev. Samuel J. May.

Dr. Lyman Clary was called to the chair, and Mr. P. H. Agan was made Secretary.

Mr. C. D. B. Mills moved the appointment of a committee of three to draft resolutions, and the motion being carried, the Chair appointed Messrs. C. D. B. Mills, D. P. Phelps and P. H. Agan as such committee.

The committee subsequently reported the following series of resolutions :—

Resolved, That in the death of Rev. Samuel J. May, our *Society* has lost from our midst a widely-known, greatly gifted and loved religious teacher ; one endeared to us by many and most tender associations, who was, through years reaching back to the very beginnings of our existence as a religious society, its faithful, most affectionate and devoted pastor, and who has laid us all under a debt never to be repaid, but always to be most gratefully and tenderly remembered.

Resolved, That in his death our *community* has lost one of its most public-spirited, philanthropic and generously useful citizens, magnanimous and self-sacrificing without end—and *humanity* itself the world over has lost a warm and untiring friend. Of him it may be truly said, he was a brother to all mankind.

Resolved, That the exalted virtues of our departed friend, so marked, so bounteous and so rare, deserve well to be celebrated and kept in perpetual record, and we rejoice that we may hold and commend these as the legacy he has left us, inestimably rich and precious, the imperishable possession and sacrament to be appropriated for quickening, before which all may well feel incited to seek to attain something of that high self-sacrifice and untiring devotion to human kind for which he was distinguished.

Resolved, That we tender our warm sympathies to the stricken family, the descendants and all the kindred of our brother, invoking for them the kind consolations and supports of Heaven in this their hour of sorrow, and we point them not without joy to the assurance that a soul that has wrought so faithfully and signally well, has, beyond peradventure, gone to its large reward.

Resolved, That we hereby authorize and instruct the trustees of this society, in conjunction with a committee of three, to be appointed to act in concert with them, to cause to be placed in the walls of the church, a tablet suitably inscribed to the name and memory of Mr. May.

Resolved, That a committee of five be appointed in behalf of our society to take, after conferring with the family of the deceased, and in consonance with their wishes, such steps as may be deemed requisite for providing for the funeral services.

Before the resolutions were put to vote, short and feeling addresses were made by Messrs. C. D. B. Mills, C. B. Sedgwick, S. R. Calthrop, D. P. Phelps, and H. L. Green, of the society, and on invitation, by the Rev. E. W. Mundy, and Charles E. Fitch. While none of the addresses were labored, all bore testimony to the moral and intellectual worth of the deceased, a worth indeed whose eulogy cannot find expression in words. The following committees were then appointed:—

To prepare and decorate the Church for the funeral:—H. N. White, J. H. Clark, O. V. Tracy, Mrs. Church, Mrs. E. A. Putnam, Mrs. E. P. Howlett and Mrs. D. F. Gott.

On the tablet:—Mrs. Dr. Clary, Mrs. W. B. Smith, and Mrs. O. T. Burt.

To confer with the family concerning the arrangements for the funeral:—E. B. Judson, C. B. Sedgwick, C. F. Williston, C. D. B. Mills and J. L. Bagg.

The funeral was announced to take place from the Church of the Messiah, on Thursday, July 6th, at 2 1-2 P. M., and the meeting adjourned.

SOCIETY OF CONCORD.

The following resolutions, adopted by the members of a Jewish congregation, are so honorable to them, and express so feelingly the common sentiment which pervades all classes of the community, that we make them an exception, and give them a place in this memorial.

At a special meeting of the Society of Concord, in Syracuse, held at the vestry rooms on the evening of July 5th, the death of the late Rev. Mr. May was announced, and a committee on resolutions appointed, consisting of Messrs. Jacob Straus, I. Henry Danziger and Bernhard Bronner. The committee reported the following preamble and resolutions, which were unanimously adopted by the meeting:—

Whereas, It has pleased our Almighty Father to call hence to a better life in heaven our esteemed fellow citizen, the Rev. Samuel J. May, be it therefore

Resolved, That in the death of the Rev. Samuel J. May, the State has lost one of its most eminent citizens, the community one of its truest philanthropists, the church one of its most liberal pillars, and mankind at large the noblest specimen of a man, who devoted his life to all that is pure and holy in the eyes of God and man.

Resolved, That while we bow in humble submission to the decrees of Providence, we hereby extend our heartfelt sympathies to the bereaved relatives of the deceased.

Resolved, That this Society in a body, attend the funeral obsequies of the lamented departed.

Resolved, That these proceedings be placed on our record and published in the daily papers of the city, and that a copy duly engrossed be handed to the bereaved relatives of the deceased.

FUNERAL SERVICES.

On the morning of Thursday, July 6th, there was a private service at Mr. Wilkinson's house. Rev. Frederic Frothingham read appropriate passages of Scripture. Rev. W. P. Tilden prayed, and Mr. A. Bronson Alcott made an address of indescribable beauty, delicacy and tenderness. Not long afterwards the household re-assembled to listen to the reminiscences of Mr. George B. Emerson, Rev. W. P. Tilden, and others. Mr. Emerson spoke of his early and ever-growing love for Mr. May, of their college-life, and of the delightful Sunday evenings which he had spent with him at Col. May's house in Boston. Mr. Emerson stated that Mr. May received his first anti-slavery impressions from Daniel Webster's denunciation of the Slave Trade, and his eloquent allusion to the duty of the pulpit to speak out concerning its sin and shame, in his memorable oration at Plymouth. Mr. Emerson believes that in going to Brooklyn, Conn., and declining calls to other places, Mr. May was governed by the consideration that in worldly goods it was the poorest parish, and less likely to obtain a desirable pastor.

In accordance with a very generally expressed wish that it should be so done, the body enclosed in a metallic casket, was, at 10 o'clock, removed to the Church of the Messiah, which loving hands had fittingly decorated, and placed before the pulpit, from which he had spoken so many faithful and earnest words. The doors of the Church were opened, and from that hour until the time appointed for the service, great numbers of persons of all classes, conditions and creeds, came forward to take a last look of that benevolent, loving face, and pay their last respects to the venerated friend. Every seat in the church that had not been reserved for the family and pall-bearers was occupied some time before the hour appointed for the services. The porch was crowded, and the stairway and yard outside were also filled with the old and the young, the rich and the poor, all eager to join in doing honor to the name and memory of the beloved dead. On either side of the altar were seated the city and other attending clergy, and in slips in front were the members of the Board of Education, of which Mr. May was for several years President. Inside of the altar sat four aged pall-bearers, who were personal friends: George Wansey, Captain Hiram Putnam, Joseph Savage and E. B. Culver. At ten minutes before three o'clock the family and friends entered the church preceded by the officiating clergy and other pall-bearers,— Mayor F. E. Carroll, E. B. Judson, C. B. Sedgwick, James L. Bagg, Dr. H. B. Wilbur, Hon. Dennis McCarthy, Dr. Lyman Clary and N. F. Graves. The pulpit was occupied by Rev. S. R. Calthrop, William Lloyd Garrison, Bishop Loguen, C. D. B. Mills and Rev. T. J. Mumford.

SERVICES AT THE CHURCH.

As the procession entered the church, the organ, at which

Prof. Ernest Held presided, gave forth a voluntary, after which the choir sang

"Cast thy burden on the Lord,
And He will sustain thee and comfort thee."

Rev. S. R. Calthrop then offered prayer.

Infinite Father, God of light and love, we are assembled here to-day to thank Thee for everything. We bless Thy name for the beautiful world Thou has given us. We thank Thee for all the kindly relations between man and man, and for the tender family ties that Thou hast given us. Here, in the midst of tears, we bless Thee for death; for that beautiful angel of Thine whom Thou dost send to each of us in turn, saying, with silent and gentle voice, "Son or daughter, come up higher!" And so, O Father, while many hearts shall feel a weariness to-day, and all shall feel that something noble has gone out of the world, we, nevertheless, with the spirit of him who lies here, bless Thy name that Thou hast received him to Thyself. He loved Thee in this world, and did try with all the might that was in him to do Thy will here. He saw Thy face here, and rejoiced in it, and would that all men would rejoice in the same. Father we bless Thee for the benediction of his life and thank Thee that Thou didst put it into his heart to be such an one. In the name of him who lies silent before us, we bless Thee for the true and beautiful influences that taught him to be a Christian and a true man. Above all, in duty to him, we thank Thee for the beautiful manifestations of love that he saw in Jesus Christ. We thank Thee for all that Jesus was to him personally. We thank Thee that the shadow of that beautiful cross fell on his life, a mingled command and benediction, and that he took it up and carried it all his days. We thank Thee, Father in heaven, that as Jesus was so he strove to be in this world; with humble heart, never thinking that he had obtained, nevertheless, pressing toward the mark ever. We thank Thee that Thou didst put it into his heart to love the poor that Jesus loved; that he did take up the cause of the oppressed as a precious legacy from the Master's hand; that he desired ever, as Jesus did, to go about doing good; to put down the kingdom of wrong, and to establish the kingdom of right ; to minister to the poor, the fatherless, the oppressed and them that had no helper. We thank Thee for the large, noble heart of this man, who said that all mankind was his brother. We pray Thee, dear Father, that, as the light has been so plainly manifested before us, we may be led to love it more ourselves, lest town and country may feel shrunken because one just man has gone. O, Father, send down his spirit upon us, and grant that we may take up the work just where he laid it down, with thanksgiving to Thee that we are for Thy sake, and for man's to do it. We thank Thee for all these things, in the name of him who was the leader, the teacher, the brother of him, who has gone up higher.

Rev. T. J. Mumford, of Dorchester, Massachusetts, one of Mr. May's early students, read appropriate selections of Scripture.

The Rev. Mr. Calthrop gave out, and the choir sang the 376th hymn.*

> While thee I seek, protecting Power !
>   Be my vain wishes stilled ;
> And may this consecrated hour
>   With better hopes be filled.
>
> Thy love the powers of thought bestowed ;
>   To thee my thoughts would soar ;
> Thy mercy o'er my life has flowed—
>   That mercy I adore !
>
> In each event of life, how clear
>   Thy ruling hand I see !
> Each blessing to my soul more dear,
>   Because conferred by thee.

*This Hymn, and all the other Hymns read and sung during the services, were favorites of Mr. May's, and were selected for the occasion on that account.

Addresses were then made by Mr. C. D. B. Mills and others, as follows :

We are here together to-day, friends, to testify to one common grief. All are mourners, each one carries in his bosom sense of personal bereavement.

We have come, not as is often the wont, as outside friends or neighbors, to gather around a stricken family in the hour of their sorrow, to offer our respect to the memory of a deceased acquaintance, and perform the last offices for one who, however well regarded or even in general way esteemed, was of no near relation or special importance to us. No, we are here ourselves as one bereaved family. Our several households have been entered, our several circles broken, our community, society itself, has suffered a deep, an irreparable loss, and every heart feels the pang of the separation. All ages grieve, the children with the adults, for this brother was not less dear to the heart of tenderest childhood than to the intelligence, the affection of maturest years. If only those who were simply friends were to speak on this occasion, sympathizers, not mourners, I think no lips would be opened here to day. And beyond the bounds of this large congregation, there is another, far larger, un-gathered, unseen to the eye, but one with us in feeling, in sense of the deep and overbearing sorrow.

For a great soul has departed, one widely related and deeply knit to human hearts, wherever seen and known. What a generous nature was his, that went out in devotion and love to all his kind, that was friend to humanity, and drew in warmest sympathy and ceaseless kindly office to all subjects of suffering, or of want or of sorrow! His love was universal, and it never chilled, never wearied. Nothing could discourage or alienate him, or reduce his faith in the good possibilities. The instances of his fine benefactions, his aid by counsel and by hand, for most part silent and unknown save to the subject and himself, in our city alone, no one now can begin to enumerate, and probably in full they will never be known to any. Many and many a one he has saved from sense of friendlessness, from the hard pressures, from discouragement and surrender to the fearful temptations. He kept open door, he spread bountiful table, freely inviting all the poor and heavy laden, and none who came went empty away. We hear that of the Indian Logan, chief of the Mingoes in the last century, sitting quietly in his home, and refusing all participation in the wars which his countrymen waged against the whites, the red men were wont to say as they passed the cabin, There dwells the friend of the white man. I think that through all these years, upon the door of that house on yonder slope, might have been written, Here dwells the friend *of all men.*

This man has left no real estate behind, but I deem the estate he does leave is far more real than any lands or structures that earth affords. He has left no iron safe well filled with bonds, with scrips of stocks accounted of such value among men, but the stocks he transmits are far more precious and enduring, deposited in stronger safe,—the human heart. So rich a man, leaving such legacies of wealth, not for one or for few, but for all, has never died from our midst before.

His charity beginning at home and doing all possible in the humble every day relations, did not stop there. His benevolence was diffusive and wide reaching as the race.

The broad humanities of his soul brought him inevitably into connection with the great reforms of the time, particularly the Anti-Slavery, Temperance and Woman's Rights. One of the very first to espouse the cause of the slave, as one here present* doubtless will tell you, more fitly and fully than I can, he labored with unswerving devotion and at great personal cost to the end. His earnest unsparing appeals, his urgent, hearty incitements to duty, have been among the most effective in this memorable anti-slavery conflict. And when at length emancipation came, he was alert to meet promptly its responsibilities ; he gave freely his energies and his substance to provide for the education and enlightenment of the newly freed. Any enterprise that sought the improvement of man found in him a cordial friend and helper ; he labored for prison reform, for peace, for popular education, for the reclamation by kindliest methods of juvenile offenders, for the interests of the working man, just wages to all, to man and to woman alike for all faithful performance. And with all this he was a most untiring and devoted preacher and pastor, an honor to the denomination to which he belonged, a constant powerful worker everywhere in behalf of religious enlightenment and emancipation, for a true and liberal faith, and most of all a noble worthy life.

But a warm quenchless benevolence and spirit of generous self-sacrifice, were not our brother's sole characteristic. He held in blending with them other qualities which went to temper and perfect them, and built up one harmonious, balanced, perfect character. With all the fine sensibilities, the tenderness, affection, and deeply sensitive nature of woman, he united those traits, which, essential to all strength

* Mr. Garrison.

and completeness, belong more particularly to the severer temperament of man. He had stern, unblenching courage. He knew not shrinking or fear. In presence of danger or overawing threat he could be, he always was, as upstanding and unmoved as a soldier. In his urgent advocacy of the cause of the slave, he was not seldom brought into relations of exposure, sometimes of imminent personal peril, yet such a thing as intimidation or surrender was never in his thought. I have seen him when assailed,

> " Patient and meek he stood ;
> His foes ungrateful, sought his life—
> He labored for their good."
> " The sandal tree, most sacred tree of all,
> Perfumes the very axe which bids it fall."

And to more dangerous influences, bland seductions dissuasions of friends, that would tone down his zeal and withdraw him from undivided devotion to this path, which to him was the path of duty, albeit beset with many thorns, his ear was deaf. His heart loving and tender everywhere, here was steel. Such fine poise and blending of the different qualities, such happy union of the elements that make up fullness and strength of character, is very seldom found.

It did not seem to us that he could ever die. His aims implied an unending activity among us, and his labors were part of the plan of the world ; they took hold on the forever. The familiar beaming face, the musical accents of the voice—we counted upon them as confidently to be ours at short intervals as the rising of the sun or the courses of the seasons. Why should so loved and inspiring a sight, so indispensable to our own life and quickening, ever go away ?

And yet we knew also that death must come.

"By cool Siloam's shady rill,
The lily must decay."

And this lily of human life, the lily man, fairest of all the blooms that ever put forth from the bosom of the earth, —this must full quickly fade and perish. Death has taken this fine flower also for its own, and we can see and know it no more. We have now henceforth to speak in the past tense. The wistful, anxious thought asks, Why; asks, Where, O where brother, art thou gone, but the eternities are silent.

We know that his life had solidity with the foundation of the heavens, that he cannot drop out of the universe, that wherever worlds are with their laws of justice, benefi-cence, love, there he dwells at home ; that wherever and whatever he be, he is in the bosom and warm embrace of the infinite Love. For his spirit here was lovingly set to the music of the skies, he was wedded to the everlasting.

Too grateful we cannot be that he remained with us so long, that for more than a quarter of a century our city has had the light of that saintly presence, pouring its benigni-ties into all eyes, shedding the dawn of worthier ambitions, some touch of nobler aspirations and better resolve into every heart. Who will not give thanks for all that had to do with introducing him here, the religious society that invited, the friends that encouraged, the influences that de-termined his choice? Who will not bless those ances-tors, the John May that in youth migrated and settled at Roxbury, the Sewalls and Quincys of the olden days, that they so wed, so bore and reared offspring, that in due time there' might be such parentage to fruit in such a son? Who not bless that quiet, but most sterling and accomplished mother, leaving so deeply the stamp of her affection upon him; that kindly father, "warden of King's Chapel," who with such care and skill guided the tender years, watchful to encourage, not to cross or mar the generous instincts, to bring out to full and perfect bloom this delicate, noble flower? We all had stake there, my friends, and the following future lay wrapped up in those childhood days, largely in the nurture to that little boy of the courtly, but tender and loving father.

But an end to eulogy. It easily becomes excessive and in effect harmful, resting absorbed in the person rather than regarding the character, dwelling in the history rather than the idea, the reality greater than history, which transcends all. This mortal has put on immortality. We have to do now with the ethereal. Samuel J. May was of worth to us most especially, not for what he historically was, but for what in him was hinted, tor the intimation we saw there of the infinite and unseen. There was symbolism and the worth was in the thing behind the symbol. Any scripture, the highest and largest, is but a fragment of the universal volume. The divinest souls that have lived were but broken lights through which shone, somewhat refracted and diffracted withal, a little ray, a tiny beam of the effulgence and the beauty of God. Jesus was but a hint of the unexplored and unimagined possibilities.

It was to intimate to us something of this that our friend came. He was sent from God. It was a repast to which we were invited, furnished in most bountiful profusion, every nourishment, every delicacy. Our brother *gave himself* to us, in mystic sense his own body and blood, all that he had or was, that we might eat not to enjoy and to slumber, but to gather strength wherewith to rise up and

do. It was an evening's entertainment at the house of a
friend, where the conversation of the guest that had dropped
in was so fine, we were transported, lifted and ravished
away; the long hours were beguiled, and ere we were aware
the night was spent. We deemed that an angel had spoken
to us, and so it was.

> "He spoke and words more soft than rain,
> Brought back the age of gold again ;
> His actions won such reverence sweet,
> As hid all measure of the feat."

But our stranger guest, mysteriously coming, mysteriously disappearing, has gone, and we look for him farther in
vain. As the lightning, which appeareth in the east, shin-
eth unto the west for the instant, so also is the coming of
the son of man. That memorable evening is past, the
crisp morning is upon us, and we are bidden, man, woman,
each for most part alone, forth and abroad to translate and
to realize.   .

God's volume of revelation and of message is never
closed. We have read of these things in books, great deeds,
saintly divine lives, souls that made earth celestial, have
heard them celebrated in poetry and song, treasured them
in our imagination and beheld them as of days more glorious, more blessed than ours. They were not to be in the
realities of our experience. They were of the romance that
glowed in the ages long departed. But this man, modest,
unassuming, claiming nothing, professing only to be a humble follower of Jesus, treading at remote distance in his
footprints,—in respect to the great qualities, in sweetness,
poise, love and self-sacrifice, certainly approximated if he
did not equal that Master, who to his thought was peerless.
The life seemed to itself so unsufficing, so infinitely short of
its own ideal. Yet we now can see, remembering withal

the human limitations, that here again the heavens have bended to the earth.

I have heard that this earth is ameliorating, that however slowly, surely, consuming if need be untold æons of time, it is moving to its destiny, to become purified and ripened, finely fit for the abode of man. That the volcanos are becoming extinct, are less numerous and less violent to-day than of old, that the nether explosive fires are burning out. That compensating, absorbing agencies are at work, neutralizing the poisons, and rendering more wholesome and life-sustaining the air. Recent science tells us that certain fragrant essences, that fine blooms like the narcissus, heliotrope, mignonette, lily, co-operate with the strong angels phosphorus and electricity, to sweeten and vitalize the atmosphere, nay that they may disinfect the marsh, and swallow and transmute the poisonous emanations. One loves to think there must be constant advance and increase, more ozone in the air to-day, more life in the sunbeam.

So, on the moral earth too, is amelioration. Blooms of saintly souls through all the ages have purified and enriched this atmosphere, absorbed the poisons and exalted the vital conditions. Human affection has been purer and sweeter since Jesus lived and loved, and the upward way grows easier, since so many true have pressed there with eager feet, enduring the cross, despising the shame.

We also are called to work in the same glorious line. Each one of us, however narrow his sphere, may do somewhat towards the grand accomplishment. Each may be at least a humble lily of the valley, to help to renew and recover some little district of this still much infected domain.

Consecrated by this grave, reverting to the luminous life we see here,—closed now but also unclosed, transplanted, transfigured, a star in the skies henceforth.—alas for us if we feel not the heavenly quickening, if we rise not this day to a higher devotion, a larger fervor of noble living than we had ever known or even thought before !

If I have ever coveted that rare gift of speech, whereby the deep emotions of the soul are enabled to find something like an adequate expression, I do so on this occasion. But, alas ! by no command of language can I hope to do any justice to my feelings or to your own. We are participating in common, in a great bereavement. These mourning children have lost one of the best of fathers, one of the wisest of counsellors and guides. I have lost a most affectionate and unswerving friend, an early and untiring co-worker in the broad field of freedom and humanity, a brother beloved incomparably beyond all blood relationship. Syracuse has lost one of its most useful and esteemed citizens ; the nation one of the worthiest of its sons ; the world one of the purest, most philanthrophic, most divinely actuated of all its multitudinous population. In him all the elements of goodness, mercy and truth were so equally blended as to form a character as perfect and beautiful as it is in the scope of ages to produce. What could surpass his habitual gentleness and tenderness of spirit, the modesty of his nature, his self-abnegation, his moral intrepidity, in times of fiery trial, his inflexible adherence to fundamental principles, his ready espousal of every righteous cause, in conflict with a corrupt overmastering public sentiment, his compassionate sympathy for every phase of human degradation and misery, his generous disposition to relieve the necessities of the poor and needy, his varied labors to establish the kingdom of righteousness in the earth ? Like Job, " he was a perfect and upright man, one who feared God,

and eschewed evil; so that when the ear heard him, it blessed him; when the eye saw him, it gave witness to him;
because he delivered the poor that cried, and the fatherless,
and him that had none to help him. The blessings of him
that was ready to perish, came upon him; and he caused
the widow's heart to sing for joy. He was eyes to the blind,
and feet was he to the lame, and the cause which he knew
not, he searched out." Never was a portraiture more ac-
curately drawn than this; and if our departed friend had
been the first to sit for it, it could not have been more strikingly exact in all its lineaments. Some of his other dis-
tinguishing characteristics are felicitously portrayed by
Wordsworth, in his description of the " Happy Warrior,"
as one

> " Who comprehends his trust, and to the same
> Keeps faithful with a singleness of aim ;
> And therefore does not stop, nor lie in wait
> For wealth or honor, or for worldly state ;
> Whom they must follow: on whose head must fall,
> Like showers of manna, if they come at all ;
> Whose powers shed round him in the common strife,
> Or mild concerns of ordinary life,
> A constant influence, a peculiar grace ;
> But who, if he be called upon to face
> Some awful moment to which heaven has joined
> Great issues, good or bad, for human kind,
> Is happy as a lover ; and attired
> With sudden brightness, like a man inspired ;
> And, through the heat of conflict, keeps the law
> In calmness made, and sees what he foresaw ;
> Or if an unexpected call succeed,
> Come when it will, is equal to the deed ;
> Whom neither shape of danger can dismay,
> Nor thought of tender happiness betray ;
> Who, whether praise of him must walk the earth
> For ever, and to noble deeds give birth,
> Or he must go to dust without his fame,
> And leave a dead, unprofitable name,

Finds comfort in himself and in his cause;
And, while the mortal mist is gathering, draws
His breath in confidence of Heaven's applause;—
This is the happy warrior; this is he
Whom every man in arms should wish to be."

Such, in the very letter and spirit, was SAMUEL JOSEPH
MAY. Witness half a century of active participation in all
the leading reforms of the age! Witness the temptations,
trials, sacrifices, perils to which he willingly subjected himself in the service of the enslaved millions at the South,
until it was granted unto him to see their fetters broken
and to join with them in singing the song of jubilee!

It is now more than forty years since I made his acquaintance, and happily secured his friendship, the value of which
to me, subsequently, proved to be beyond all price. I shall
always gratefully remember that he was among the very
earliest to take me by the hand, and bid me God speed in
my labors for the immediate and unconditional abolition of
American Slavery. In his printed " Recollections of the
Anti-Slavery Conflict," he generously acknowledges his
deep indebtedness to me on hearing my first lectures on
slavery in Boston, in the autumn of 1830—adding that they
gave a new direction to his thoughts—a new purpose to his
ministry. However that may have been, I am sure that I
have felt far more indebted to him; for, without his encouraging words and zealous co-operation, I should have
lost much of the inspiration that enabled me to battle per-
sistently against all opposing forces. At that time, the
pastor of a small Unitarian church in Brooklyn, Conn., and
the occupant of the only Unitarian pulpit in that State, he
had no slight cross to bear, no inconsiderable amount of theological odium to confront on account of his alledged doctrin-
al heresies; and he therefore might have plausibly pleaded

that he had already as heavy a load as he could well carry, without esponsing any other disreputable issue. But it was not in his nature to consult expediency where duty was plainly revealed: nor to measure the amount of proscription he was willing to bear for righteousness sake. If it must be so, he was ready to be branded as a fanatic or an incendiary, as he had been a heretic. No "son of thunder" was he, indeed, but eminently a "son of consolation;" yet to the mildness of a John, he united the firmness and moral courage of a Paul, when called to meet the solemn issues of the times. Avoiding all violations of good taste, and wisely circumspect in his utterances, he nevertheless could speak in such tones of rebuke and warning as to make the ears of hardened transgressors tingle, and at the same time was quick to perceive where simple entreaty might be effectually substituted for harsh impeachment. He had no taste for controversy as such; no man disliked it more. "As much as he lieth in you, live peacefully with all men," was with him a favorite apostolic injunction; and he continually overflowed with the milk of human kindness. But he felt none the less sensibly the obligation to "declare the whole counsel of God," as revealed to his own soul, whether men would hear or whether they would forbear. What he sought to know, was the truth; what he stood ready at all odds to maintain, was the right. If he was a heretic, he had still unwavering faith in God; if he was on any occasion a disturber of the peace, it was only in the sense in which prophets and apostles, saints and martyrs have been; if he stood in a minority, sometimes alone, it was because he could not be tempted by any consideration to go with the multitude to do evil. His standard of judgment was very simple, and, so far as speculative theology was concerned, broadly catholic. "I ask not," to quote his own language,

" what may be a man's profession or faith; I ask not what may be a man's creed or system of theology; I ask only whether he gives unequivocal evidence of his fidelity to God, and his love of the Father, by his fidelity to the right, and his love of the brethren, *especially his poor brethren*." And, truly, in the light of such an example as he set, of such a life as he lived, how worthless is every sectarian shibboleth! Men are to be known by their fruits, not by their professions; and what a prolific fruit-bearer was here!

> " For modes of faith let graceless zealots fight ;
> His can't be wrong whose life is in the right."

If ever there was " an Israelite indeed, in whom there was no guile," he existed in the person of him whose mortal remains lie before us. I can conceive of no society beyond the grave, however pure and exalted, into which he may not enter, and be received as a worthy guest—aye, as a brother beloved, and a member of the household of saints " in good and regular standing." Let it be remembered that if the same averment had been made of the great Founder of Christianity in his day, it would have been deemed shocking impiety by all who made any pretensions to soundness of religious faith; for was not he, also, a heretic—aye, of the worst type? Had he not eaten with publicans and sinners? Did he not audaciously impeach the piety of priest and Levite, and recognize as worthy of imitation and praise a hated, heretical Samaritan? Had he not been convicted of blasphemy? Had he not a devil?

For myself—raising here no question as to whose theological opinions are sound or unsound—I feel that, as the fearless advocate of liberty of conscience, as against all dogmatic authority and ecclesiastic rule, Mr. May is entitled to our common gratitude ; for, however dissimilar we may be in our scriptural interpretations or religious convictions, he contended for us all equally as for himself. Like the Apostle, he regarded it as a small matter to be judged of man's judgment. Like that same heroic spirit, he inculcated the duty of proving all things in an independent investigation, every one for himself ; taking care to hold fast that which is good. Like a greater than Paul, he asked, " Why judge ye not of yourselves what is right ? " Perhaps to no one in our country is the cause of free inquiry, in its broadest signification, more indebted than to this world-embracing friend and brother.

Mark Antony lamenting over the dead body of Cæsar, exclaims :—

> " The Evil that men do lives after them ;
> The good is oft interred with their bones."

Of the truthfulness of his first assertion there can be no question. The evil that men do survives their earthly existence, and not unfrequently goes down from generation to generation. But by what law of Providence does it happen that the good is ever buried with their bones? Believe not the statement. Evil has no such advantage over good. The same conditions, the same chances, the same limitations apply to each ; but what a difference in quality ! For,

> "Only the actions of the just
> Smell sweet, and blossom in the dust."

Yes, even in the dust they blossom, and bear fruit abundantly for the nourishment of a long line of posterity. Beautifully has the great master of poetry illustrated this diffusive power of goodness in the oft-quoted couplet—

> " How far the little candle throws its beams !
> So shines a good deed in the naughty world."

And it retains its lustre long after the removal of the mind that conceived and the hand that executed it.

What one of the multitudinous good acts of our beloved friend, what one of the many grand testimonies uttered by him with such boldness and fidelity, can possibly become extinct in his grave? These have entered into the general life of the community; they have widely affected the popular conscience and heart; they have greatly lessened, and will continue to lessen, the sum of human sorrow and wretchedness; they have powerfully contributed towards shaping the destiny of the nation. "Though dead, he yet speaketh;" and his spirit still walks abroad in all its quickening power.

With what zeal and persistency did he give himself to the cause of popular education, with all its far-reaching consequences, from the primary school to the university! How well he comprehended its priceless value to the millions, its indispensable necessity to the maintenance of free institutions! As the natural sequence to his anti-slavery labors, how deep was the interest he evinced in the instruction of the benighted freedmen of the South! No one ever responded more warmly to the Divine mandate, "Let there be light," than himself.

To that most blessed and fundamentally important movement which seeks the abolishment of the drinking customs of society, he gave an early adhesion and an earnest support. Alas! that these pernicious customs still prevail so widely, carrying with them a legion of evils! Yet, had it not been for the temperance reformation, the land would have been given over to intoxication beyond all reasonable hope of recovery. It has brought sunshine and joy, and health and happiness, to tens of thousands of homes, and

saved millions from the liability of going down to drunk-
ards' graves. It has greatly diminished insanity, pauper-
ism and crime, strengthened private and public virtue,
accelerated the general prosperity, and augmented the national wealth. Still, it needs all possible encouragement
and support; for the obstacles thrown in the pathway of its
complete success continue to be of a formidable nature.
The departure, therefore, of one whose example and testimony were so efficient in its behalf, is a very serious loss.

" Blessed are the peacemakers ; for they shall be called
the children of God." If I mistake not, the very first re-
formatory movement which challenged the attention and
won the advocacy of Mr. May, was that for the promotion
of universal peace. This must have been nearly half a century ago, at the very commencement of his ministerial
career. Aside from the teachings ot Jesus, to no one probably was he so indebted for his deep-seated convictions on
this subject, as to the venerable Noah Worcester, of blessed
memory. His whole being seemed to be permeated with
the divine element of peace, as was the Saviour's whom he
loved and revered so profoundly, and whose example he
constantly held up as worthy of all imitation. His spirit
was ever attuned to the angelic song, " Glory to God in the
highest ; on earth peace ; good will towards men." Peace
radiated from his countenance—found fitting cadence in the
music of his voice—made fragrant his daily walk and conversation. While he clearly saw that, in the Divine Providence, war had both its admonitory and retributive uses,
he saw not less clearly that

" Were half the power that fills the world with terror,
    Were half the wealth bestowed on camps and courts,
Given to redeem the human mind from error,
    There were no need of arsenals or forts.

The warrior's name would be a name abhorred :
And every nation that should lift again
Its head against a brother, on its forehead
Would wear forever more the curse of Cain."

That, just prior to his being summoned hence, he was permitted to hear of the ratification of an honorable treaty of peace between Great Britain and the United States, whereby all their grave difficulties are to be amicably settled, must have given to him inexpressible gratification, causing a feeling kindred to that of aged Simeon, when he exclaimed, " Lord, let now thy servant depart in peace ; for mine eyes have seen thy salvation." In view of all the circumstances, it is the most cheering event in the history of international arbitration, and cannot fail to exercise a salutary influence upon the nations of the earth in the bloodless adjustment of their variances with each other. In that case, it will be a long stride towards the goal of universal peace, which, whenever reached, shall be the fulfillment of the inspiring prediction—

" No more shall nation against nation rise,
Nor ardent warriors meet with hateful eyes :
Nor fields with gleaming steel be covered o'er,
The brazen trumpets kindle rage no more ;
But useless lances into scythes shall bend,
And the broad falchion in a ploughshare end.
Then palaces shall rise ; the joyful son
Shall finish what his short-lived sire begun ;
Their vines a shadow to their race shall yield,
And the same hand that sow'd, shall reap the field."

Farewell—at the longest, a brief farewell—friend of liberty, of temperance, of peace, of universal brotherhood, of equal rights for the whole human race, without distinction of clime, color, sex or nationality !

Farewell, lover of God and of man, without partiality

and without hypocrisy—ready for every good word and work—benefactor of the poor and outcast, succorer of the hunted fugitive slave, sympathizer with the widow and orphan in their distress, rescuer of the wandering and lost, strengthener of the weak, and lifter up of the bowed down !

Farewell, sweetest, gentlest, most loving and most loved of men !

"Gone to the Heavenly Father's rest !
    The flowers of Eden round thee blowing,
And on thine ear the murmurs blest
    Of Shiloah's water softly flowing !
Beneath that Tree of Life which gives
To all the earth its healing leaves !
In the white robe of angels clad ;
    And wandering by that sacred river,
Whose streams of holiness make glad
    The city of our God forever !

Gentlest of spirits !—not for thee
    Our tears are shed, our sighs are given ;
Why mourn to know thou art a free
    Partaker of the joys of Heaven ?
Finish'd thy work, and kept thy faith
In Christian firmness unto death ;
And beautiful as sky and earth,
    And Autumn's sun in downward going,
The blessed memory of thy worth
    Around thy place of slumber glowing !"

ADDRESS OF BISHOP LOGUEN OF THE AFRICAN M. E. CHURCH.

I would not tax your patience for one moment were it not for the intimate relationship that has existed between this dear friend and myself for over a quarter of a century. I had commenced laboring for my people here—the colored race—a few years before the Rev. Mr. May came to this village, as it was then. It was a dark place,—no friends, no encouragement, a solitary wilderness for the colored man. I began my labors as a poor boy, teaching school here ; and I shall never forget the joy that our dear friend brought me when I made his acquaintance. From that hour until his death, I never met him, in the darkest moment, or amid the most fearful trials of my people, but that a ray of sunlight would strike my breast from his countenance.

While these friends have been speaking of him, I have been thinking of all the oppressed and afflicted he has relieved and comforted. Those who have known him as long as I have, can say that there are no words that can exalt him as a man and as a brother of humanity. He was a brother to all. I feel like weeping with his friends and his children. He was as dear to me as any one could be. Never did I go to his house for counsel, or for help in vain. Enemies were prowling around, but he was always true and always ready to befriend and welcome me to his table, to his study, and to his fireside. He was truly a friend to humanity, everywhere, and under all circumstances of life. As one of the colored race I can testify heartily that he was a brother to us as well as others. If I could say all that was in my heart I would say much more ; but you have heard much. Being the only one of my race to stand here, I thought I must say a word about the kind heart and noble life of the dear brother lying before us. Oh! you know that a man who, twenty years ago, would prove a brother to my hated, oppressed, and enslaved people, would prove a brother to all. I can only say, God bless you my dear friends, his children and relatives, follow in his footsteps.

ADDRESS OF REV. W. P. TILDEN, OF BOSTON.

It has been said that love will always bear one word more, if it be said in simplicity and sincerity," though I should hardly dare attempt to say that word now, after all that has been said, did I not stand here as the representative of others, as well as to speak a simple word for myself. The brief notes I hold in my hand, will explain what I mean. Just before I left Boston I received these letters, one from the Rev. Charles Lowe, known to all the Unitarians in this place, and throughout the country, as the beloved Secretary of the American Unitarian Association, for some years past ; having recently resigned because of ill health to the regret of all who knew him. He says :—

MY DEAR MR. TILDEN :—I write a line to express my earnest hope that you will represent the Association, as they have asked you to, at the funeral of Mr. May. If I could go, I should accompany you, for not only is my personal feeling for him very tender and near, but I recognize so strongly his eminent service to our cause, that I should be glad by my presence to express it.

I hope if you go, you will say something publicly to testify to his connection with the association and his efficient service. He has been acting as a missionary, ever since he left the charge of his society, with only such interruption as his health or other engagements made necessary ; and the peculiar respect he had won all through the State in which his work was given, and his rare faculty of saying just the right word—enabled him to do what no one else could have done so well. He was our counsellor, and he was for the societies in his "diocese" (as he used to call it,) an adviser, an inciter to zeal, and a dear friend. If I were still Secretary of the Association I should feel that one of my best supporters was gone. Ever truly yours,

CHARLES LOWE.

The other note is from Mr. Shippen, who says :—

In requesting you to represent this Association at the funeral of Mr. May, I heartily accord with all that Mr. Lowe has just written, and hope that at Syracuse you may express, in behalf of our Association, as well as of the brotherhood of the ministry, our deep gratitude for the noble and faithful life of our beloved and departed brother. To many of us he was a father, rather; by his benignant and gracious presence illustrating to our hearts that tenderness and loving kindness toward the humblest and least of men, which our faith rejoices to ascribe to the Infinite Father as his dearest attribute.

Please express, especially to the family and friends, our heartfelt sympathy.

Very cordially yours,

RUSH R. SHIPPEN.

First let me express to the dear family of our departed brother our heartfelt and cordial sympathy, the heartfelt sympathy of the whole denomination. For who is there among us all that did not know and love your dear and honored father? And yet we have no word of condolence, but rather of congratulation, thanking God, with you, to-day, that through his loving kindness you have been blessed with such a noble father.

As to brother May's connection with the Unitarian Association, it would hardly be proper for me to say a word to-day, were it not that in his own heart he traced much of the love he bore for his fellow-men, and the interest he felt in

the great reforms of the age, to their principles early en-
graven upon his heart; and the secret of his success as a
preacher I am certain was that he so thoroughly, clear down
to the depths of his soul, believed every word that he
preached. It was that which touched people's hearts when
they heard him. They said, here is a man who really believes what he teaches; when he speaks of the fatherhood
of God, and when he speaks of the brotherhood of man we
know that he believes it, and therefore we are ready to listen
to him and bid him God speed in his work. Yes, brother
May had a deep and living conviction of the simple truths
of Unitarian Christianity. And, oh! how simple they are!
—the fatherhood of God ; the sonship of humanity ; the
brotherhood of the race; sin its own sorrow; holiness its
own sweet and blessed reward ; the upper mansions opening
right out of this world ; human love beginning here to be
perfected beyond. These were the truths that in earliest
childhood took hold of his heart ; that was the source of his
theology—to call God Father; that was the source of his
philanthropy. He really believed that God was his Father ;
he really believed that man was his brother, and he sought
to live that out. That was what made his philanthropy so
broad. It was color blind ; and it is the only kind of blind
ness that I know of that indicates a clear vision. He could
not see anything of the distinctions made by man in any of
God's creatures—it was the Divine image he saw everywhere. And so whenever he saw a human being there he
saw his brother, a child of the same Heavenly Father.

I would if I had time, tell you how well dear Brother
May was loved in other places besides Syracuse, and in
other States besides New York. You have enjoyed him
here now for twenty-six years. It seems to you, I suppose,
as if nobody loved him as you did. I tell you that where-

ever he went, there were those that loved him just as well as you. It was my privilege to be one of his parishioners thirty years ago, when he went fresh from the anti-slavery field of labor, and settled at South Scituate. I was then a young man working in a carpenter shop, but yet I longed for the Christian ministry ; yet how should I get into it? God knows whether I ever should, although I rather think he would have found a way for me—if brother May had not come like an angel of God, and taken right hold of my hand, hardened with toil, and clasped it, as only dear brother May could clasp a hand, and aided me with his counsel and sympathy. Oh, think how many have been clasped by that dear hand, and how many hearts have been cheered by that clasp! When he came to Scituate he drew us all to him by this strong human sympathy. He carried our sicknesses and bore our sorrows. And it was wonderful that, while he was so deeply interested in all these various objects of philanthropy, his personal interest for every individual in his parish was so deep and constant. Mr. Garrison has called him a "son of consolation." Oh, he was that indeed. Seldom do we see united that deep and tender sympathy, and that moral heroism which made him ready to do and dare for any cause, that he believed to be the cause of God and humanity.

I want to emphasize one thought before we go hence, that has already been mentioned sweetly and hopefully, that is, that our brother is not dead. God does not let him die even here. His influence will live in our hearts long to enkindle within us something of the light that shone through him for God and humanity. Of all the men that I have ever known, I do not recall one who has so fully, as I think, realized the words of the poet—

> " I live to hold communion."

But it is because our brother lived those glorious truths, that now that he has risen, he has taken up all our hearts with him.

The 271st Hymn was then read by Rev Mr. Calthrop and sung by the choir :

Awake, my soul ! stretch every nerve,
    And press with vigour on :
A heavenly race demands thy zeal,
    And an immortal crown.

A cloud of witnesses around
    Hold thee in full survey :
Forget the steps already trod,
    And onward urge thy way.

'Tis God's all-animating voice
    That calls thee from on high ;
'Tis his own hand presents the prize
    To thine aspiring eye ;

That prize with peerless glories bright,
    Which shall new lustre boast,
When victors' wreaths and monarchs' gems
    Shall blend in common dust.

Prayer was then offered by Rev. Frederick Frothingham, of Buffalo, after which the choir sung,

Nearer, my God, to thee,
    Nearer to thee :
Even though it be a cross
    That raiseth me,
Still all my song shall be,
Nearer, my God, to thee,
    Nearer to thee.

Though like a wanderer,
    The sun gone down,
Darkness be over me,
    My rest a stone,
Yet in my dreams I'd be
    Nearer to thee.

There let the way appear
  Steps unto heaven ;
All that thou sendest me
  In mercy given,
Angels to beckon me
Nearer my God, to thee,
  Nearer to thee.

Then with my waking thoughts,
  Bright with thy praise,
Out of my stony griefs,
  Bethel I'll raise ;
So by my woes to be
Nearer, my God, to thee,
  Nearer to thee.

Or if on joyful wing,
  Cleaving the sky,
Sun, moon, and stars forgot,
  Upward I fly,—
Still all my song shall be,
Nearer, my God, to thee,
  Nearer to thee.

Rev. Mr. Calthrop announced the close of the services, and said that those especially who had been unable to gain admission to the church, would be glad to know that there were to be short services at the grave, to attend which they were most cordially invited. He pronounced the benediction.

FROM THE CHURCH TO THE CEMETERY.

The casket was brought from the church between two rows of Sunday school children, stationed on the right and left from the church entrance to the hearse, all dressed in white, presenting a beautiful sight. The procession was formed, and the long line of carriages moved through James and Salina streets to Oakwood Cemetery.

AT THE GRAVE.

On arriving at the cemetery, the procession passed up the winding roadway to the place of burial, the Sunday school children again forming in two lines. A large number of people had congregated, and after the casket was taken from the hearse, brief services were held, commencing with the children singing :—

> " In the sweet by and by,
> We shall meet on that beautiful shore."

Remarks were made by the Rev. Mr. Calthrop, President Andrew D. White, of Cornell University, Rev. Mr. Mumford, and the Rev. E. W. Mundy.

REMARKS OF REV. S. R. CALTHROP.

When an Egyptian king died, his body lay in state before the assembly of the people, who were called upon solemnly to pronounce their verdict on his character. If that verdict was adverse, he was buried apart, as unworthy of honorable sepulture ; if favorable, he was buried, amid the tears of the people, among the sacred sepulchres of the kings.

We are assembled here, to pronounce our last judgment on the clay that lies before us. Here, among the leafy trees, the joyful light, and the thousand sweet sounds of summer, the dust will lie. But where shall we bury him in our hearts ? Already judgment has been passed in other places. This morning his nearest kindred,—those who had known his innermost life,—gathered, and with one voice declared, that this was the truest, kindest, faithfulest friend, father, man, their eyes had ever seen. With sweet, cheerful converse, they delighted to recall every word he had spoken, every thing he had done. 'Twas not a funeral, it was a beautiful commemoration service, which made their hearts glad.

Their verdict was, "The memory of the just is blessed." This afternoon a mourning crowd gathered, of their own accord, in the midst of the busy day, publicly to do honor to one who 'had fought a good fight, and finished his course.' Their verdict was, " O, God, we thank Thee that this man has lived." And now we, too, are gathered together, to declare, under the eye of Heaven, what our thought is. Every one is free to speak. We are not afraid to hear the testimony of any man on earth. Is there any here present, who can say that this man's ear was ever closed to any single cry of distress, of loneliness, of oppression, of poverty, of any human misery? That any just cause ever languished for lack of his help? Was there ever one a stranger, that he took not in ; naked, that he did not strive to clothe ; sick and in prison, that he did not visit? Whenever I came down the hill, from a visit to that most hospitable house, if I chanced to meet any specially forlorn man or woman going up, I was instantly sure whither they were bound. When going home, last Monday, after our church meeting, I got out of the car with an Indian. As we were walking the same way, I thought I would try an experiment, and see if this chance-met stranger knew anything about Mr. May. I inquired. " Oh," said he, " the best friend our nation ever had. I had a deaf and dumb boy nine years old. Mr. May got him into the Asylum in New York. They said, he only nine years old,—none under twelve can come in. But Mr. May said, ' Indian boy, Indian boy,'—He must come in." I wonder how many hundreds of just such tales could be told. Yes, our verdict is, " We will bury him among the kings because he hath done *good*."

Already the whole country, through the press, begins to pour in its tribute from all quarters. There was a time when men spake all manner of evil against him falsely, for Jesus' sake ; but already the cause is swallowed up in blessing. The verdict of America is, " The nation honors him, and weeps his loss."

One more verdict, and we have done. There is another assembly before which our friend is now standing. The general assembly and church of the first-born ; Jesus, bringer in of the new covenant. God, the judge of all men, and the spirits of just men made perfect. Can we not already, in faith, see that joyful welcome, and hear that last grand verdict pronounced, " Well done, good and faithful servant, enter thou into the joy of thy Lord !"

And now what a lesson this life teaches as to where a true ambition lies. I would invite all brave young American men to ponder it well. Here, in America, we all stand, in one sense as equals. Here we have no Dukes, Earls, Marquises or Lords, whose very names are supposed to give their possessors a right to stand before other men. And yet, the *thing*, for which alone these names, otherwise worthless, ought to stand, is here. Here lies one whose name no outward titles ever adorned, and yet the honor is all his own. Here lies one, who was Duke or Leader in the cause of man. Earl of justice, Lord of the glorious dominion of love and good will. Whoso wishes these coronets to be placed on his brow, let him go and do likewise. Young friend, you like him, can win them, if you love and hate the things he loved and hated ; he hated no man, he hated only the vice that degrades men, the intemperance that imbrutes men, the oppression that enslaves men, the sin and selfishness that destroy men. He loved the truth that enlarges, the justice that strengthens, and the love that blesses men. This is the word, which he, being dead, yet speaketh to you, to me, and to all men.

My Friends :—Here lies before us all that was mortal of the best man, the most truly *Christian* man I have ever known ; the purest, the sweetest ; the fullest of faith, hope and charity ; the most like the Master.

For nearly thirty years he has blessed us—for all these years his very presence has been a benediction to us.

I think that the first characteristic of our dear friend, which rises in the remembrance of us all, is his kindliness, his tenderness and love toward all God's creatures. How well do I remember its first revelation to me. Nearly thirty years ago, as a child in one of your public schools, I was upon a boat crowded with children on our way to celebrate the national anniversary. Into our midst came a man whom most of us had never before seen. He spoke, and instinctively we loved him. He "suffered little children to come unto him." Had his creed been recited to us by unfriendly lips, it would have doubtless scared us ; but the man was Mr. May, and his kindliness and goodness have never been clouded from that day to this.

But this quality was not mere geniality. It deepened and broadened into a great stream of Christian charity— charity to the distressed immigrant, to the African, to the Indian, to Jew and Gentile, to Catholic and Protestant, to those who differed from him, to those who reviled him.

Another striking characteristic was his courage. A few years since I was for a few days in London, hurrying homeward. The July riots had just taken place in New York, and I feared that they would spread to other cities, and in that case Mr. May's very nobleness would draw upon him the blind fury of the mob. Expressing dread of this to an

English lady, formerly a resident of Boston, she said, "Have no fear of Mr. May. He is one of the most courageous men I have ever known. I saw him withstand the old mob against anti-slavery, and I know him."

There are those here who know this quality in him. Many of you can doubtless recall with me how, for rescuing a slave, fellow citizens of ours were dragged from court to court over this State, and how thrilling it was when another great, good citizen* stood up and said publicly in that storm, "Why persecute those men? Samuel J. May and I did the deed."

Another characteristic was his patience. Few know how this was tried; not merely by the poor and needy, but by every man or woman with this or that plan of regenerating the universe; by that most trying class, whose poor glimmering spark of genius is smothered in half knowledge or absurdity or conceit. For all these his time and patience were limitless.

And to those who refused to work with him, refused to recognize him as a brother, refused to return the civility of his call, who thought it their duty to hold him up to public reprobation, and to misrepresent him—for those there was never a word of reproach. I heard him speak plaintively of this once, but not at all bitterly.

We who have grown up here, whether in other creeds or not, know something of this. Let any young man, no matter of what church, speak, no matter on what subject, and he was sure to see Mr. May in the front ranks of his audience, encouraging, looking on the bright side, strengthening him during his effort, counselling him after it.

* Gerrit Smith.

And all these and a host of other good qualities were real, and they were real because they were rooted in Christianity.

The question has been asked, was Mr. May a Christian?

My friends, there are certain parts of the Scriptures which no criticism will ever touch. Biblical students may remove this or that addition to the original text ; but the Sermon on the Mount--the " First commandment, and the second which is like unto it,"--the depiction of pure religion and undefiled by St. James,—these shall stand forever, for they are based upon eternal verity. Judged by these--judged by every utterance of the Founder of Christianity--Samuel J. May was one of the purest and most perfect of Christians.

When the Sermon on the Mount was read this afternoon, it seemed prophetic of the man. It was *not*--" Blessed are the pure in heart--who accept the thirty-nine articles ;" *not*, " Blessed are the peacemakers--who subscribe to the decrees of the Council of Trent;" *not*, " Blessed are ye when men shall revile you—provided ye agree to the Westminster catechism ;"--no. The blessings of that greatest of utterances since the world began, were without human test, and they fell upon our friend in full measure, and his life was the radiant witness of them, and we all saw them.

Yes, my friends, he was the best Christian man we have ever known. Had our Lord come on this earth again and into these streets any time in these thirty years, he was sure of one follower. Came He as black man, or red man, or the most wretched of white men, came He in rags or sores, this, our dear friend, would have known Him and followed

Him, no matter what weapons, carnal or spiritual, were hurled at the procession.

To him came the words of the Master he so fully believed in, " Inasmuch as ye have done it unto the least of one of these, ye have done it unto Me." To us come those other words, brushing away all formulas, " By their fruits shall ye know them."

My friends, I account it among the greatest of blessings that it was given me to know this man, and I shall always rejoice that on the last afternoon of his life I spent a most delightful hour with him, and bore away his blessing.

REMARKS OF REV. T. J. MUMFORD, OF DORCHESTER, MASS.

Born in Beaufort District, South Carolina, where four-fifths of the inhabitants were slaves, the son of a slaveholder, until I was twenty years old, I believed in slavery as a divine institution, and carried a bible in my pocket to defend it against all comers. When the faithful hands of noble Quaker women removed the sacred veil which had concealed the monstrous features of the system, and I saw clearly at last that it was not of celestial, but infernal origin, I soon lost all faith in my religious teachers, who seemed to declare that man was made for the church and not the church for man. I was almost drowning in a sea of skepticism, when Samuel J. May came to the town in Western New York where I lived.

As soon as I saw his radiant face and heard his sweet yet earnest voice, I felt drawn to him by a mighty magnetism. It became my first desire to share in the blessed work that he was doing, to follow him, although with feeble steps, and a great way off, in going about doing good. Since that day, all of my life that I can look back upon without regret and shame, I owe to the inspiration of his example and the power of his encouragement. No other friend has exerted such an uplifting influence upon my spirit. Therefore, I could not resist the strong attraction which has drawn me here to-day. There are many other things which I should find relief and joy in saying, but these threatening clouds admonish me to be content with reciting a hymn which expresses what is in all our minds and hearts.

Calmly, calmly lay him down !
He hath fought a noble fight ;
He hath battled for the right ;
He hath won the fadeless crown.

Memories, all too bright for tears,
Crowd around us from the past ;
He was faithful to the last,—
Faithful through long, toilsome years.

All that makes for human good,
Freedom, righteousness and truth,
These, the objects of his youth,
Unto age he still pursued.

Kind and gentle was his soul,
Yet it had a glorious might ;
Clouded minds it filled with light,
Wounded spirits it made whole.

Huts where poor men sat distressed,
Homes where death had darkly passed,
Beds where suffering breathed its last,
These he sought, and soothed, and blessed.

Hoping, trusting, lay him down ;
Many in the realms above
Look for him with eyes of love,
Wreathing his immortal crown.

Friends:—We might remain until the midnight, telling of the worth of Mr. May. But his deeds speak more potently than any words which we can utter, and our poor rhetoric is wholly inadequate to set forth his virtues. His life has been an uninterrupted beneficence. Want and sorrow never appealed to him in vain. His presence diffused continual blessings. When the unfortunate and the suffering in our city had exhausted every other means by which to obtain relief, they knew that after all else failed, they could go to Mr. May, and that he would open some way for them. In the activity of a long life, he has been counsellor and friend to us all; and now at his grave there come calmness and cheerfulness and high resolve into our hearts, as we look for the last time upon the dear dead face.

To the younger clergy of this region Mr. May has been a constant friend. He has appreciated our difficulties; he has understood our perplexities; he has cheered and strengthened us by his wise suggestions and by the contagion of his irrepressible hopefulness. We have called him Father for the love that we bear him, and now there is left to us the inheritance of his example, his spirit and his work. His influence descends upon us as a perpetual benediction.

To-day, as hour after hour the people passed along that they might look once more upon the features they loved so well, there came with the crowd an Indian. For a moment he stood quiet, and then the hard brown face broke into tears, and he sat down and sobbed like a child. That bereaved Indian expressed the feelings of us all. White people and black people and red people, learned and ignorant, old and young, poor and rich, Catholic and Protestant and Infidel,— we have a common sorrow, and drop our tears upon the grave of one who was a common friend. He knew neither sect nor color, nor nationality : but he saw in all men his brothers, and his ear was ever open to their words and his hand ever extended in their aid. The fresh generosity and beauty of his life is well symbolized in the fragrant flowers which loving hands have brought to his tomb, and the maturity and perfectness of his work is strikingly suggested in the ripened wheat sheaf which lies upon his coffin. His work is well done. His earthly life has been well lived. And his death was peaceful and bright as the setting of the sun.

The last day of his stay on earth, was one of pleasure to him and to the friends who saw him ; and with the disappearing twilight he passed into the glory of the other world. As sung by the poet,

> " He sat in peace in the sunshine
>   Till the day was almost done,
> And then at its close an angel
>   Stole over the threshold stone."

> " He folded his hands together,
>   He touched his eyelids with balm,
> And his lost breath floated upward,
>   Like the close of a solemn psalm."

THE END.

A hymn was sung, when the casket was deposited in the grave. The children then came forward, each one dropping a bouquet upon the bosom of their late and beloved pastor, friend and guide, as they passed. The services closed with a

BENEDICTION BY MR. MILLS.

So this mortal puts on immortality ; this corruptible puts on incorruption. That which was sown in weakness is raised in power.

Man, born of woman, is of few days. Like the flower of the field he fadeth, and full quickly goeth to decay. Man, the offspring of the skies, his being quenchless, is heir to the the immensities and the forever.

This our brother, whose mortal remains we now commit to the keeping of the grave, has ascended, and become seized of his estate. For well on earth, had he read and learned his horn-book for the skies.

As he enters there, beaming, devoted, and loving—all worlds open to receive him, angels rise up to greet him, the infinite bosom itself warms to welcome, to embrace him.

So, may we too live, that when to each of us, one after another, the hour shall come, we also may find death to be birth, and time but the door, that opens to us the eternities of God.

In Pace.

www.ingramcontent.com/pod-product-compliance
Lightning Source LLC
Chambersburg PA
CBHW030019030726
47499CB00008B/3049